The Sparrow, the Crow and the Pearl

Waltham Forest Libraries	
904 000 00497125	
Askews & Holts	29-Sep-2017
C428.6 CLA NEW	£215.00 per set
5521558	W

Story retold by Rosalind Kerven
Pictures by Melanie Williamson

D0774069

904 000 00497125

Once a small, brown sparrow and a big, black crow flew into a beautiful garden. They hopped around together, looking for tasty worms and maggots to eat. They chatted happily and seemed to be the very best of friends. But suddenly Crow gave a caw of excitement. He turned his back on Sparrow and spread out his wings, as if he were trying to hide something.

"Hey!" tweeted Sparrow, "What are you up to, Crow? What have you got there?"

"Nothing," Crow said quickly.

But Sparrow could tell that he was lying, for the next moment, Crow leaped forward and grabbed something in his beak. Then he flapped his wings and carried it up to the very top of the highest tree in the garden.

"Come back!" Sparrow squawked up at him.
"Show me what you've got!"

"Why should I?" Crow cawed. "It's mine!"

Sparrow ruffled her feathers. "If you were
really my friend," she grumbled, "you would
share things. At the very least, you would tell
me what it is."

Crow gave a cackle of laughter. "All right, I'll tell you, Sparrow. It's a beautiful, white pearl from an earring – a real treasure. It's much too fine for a scraggy little creature like *you* to see."

"I'm not scraggy!" cried Sparrow. "How dare you insult me? Let me see it, Crow – you beast!"

"No," cawed Crow, "never!"

Sparrow flew into a rage. She hopped up to the tree and began poking its trunk with her sharp little beak.

"Hey, Tree," she yelled, "don't let that nasty, selfish Crow sit in your branches a moment longer. Shake him out! Make him fly away!"

Tree gazed down at Sparrow. "Certainly not!" he boomed. "I'm not getting involved in your silly argument."

Sparrow exploded with anger.

"Well," she cried, "if you're too mean to help me, I shall fetch the woodcutter to chop you down!"

7

Sparrow flew like the wind to the woodcutter's house.

"Quickly, quickly!" Sparrow twittered at him. "Go and chop down the tallest tree in the garden!"

"Why should I, you silly little bird?" laughed the woodcutter. And he flicked Sparrow out of his way.

"You horrible man!" cried Sparrow. "I'm going to fetch Mouse, Mr Woodcutter. I'm going to get her to chew up your clothes as a punishment!"

8

At that very moment, Mouse poked her head out of her hole.

"What's going on?" she squeaked.

"You've got to chew up Mr Woodcutter's clothes," said Sparrow, "because he won't do what I tell him."

"Eeek, no thank you," squeaked Mouse. "I'd rather chew bread any day!" And she scuttled back inside.

"As you won't do what I say either, Mouse," Sparrow squawked after her, "I'm going to get Dog to gobble you up!"

Sparrow found Dog snoozing in his kennel at the other end of the garden.

"Wake up, Dog," she called. "I've found a nice, juicy mouse for you to eat for your dinner."

Dog opened one eye and yawned. "No thanks," he barked, "I can't stand the taste of mouse."

"That's nothing to do with me," crackled Fire. "I can't go round burning innocent sticks, Sparrow, just because you're in a bad mood."

"Oh, so that's how it is, is it?" squawked Sparrow. "Well, since you won't help me either, Fire, I'm getting the Sea to come and put you out!"

Sparrow zoomed out of the window,
out of the garden, across the forest and
down to the beach. There she found Sea
playing wave-games in the sand,
rushing in and drizzling out again.

Sea! Sea!

"Sea, Sea!" cried Sparrow. "It's time to stop
playing. I've got an important job for you. Go
ashore to the house that stands in the beautiful
garden. Hurry inside, and find Fire.
Then pour yourself over him and
put him out."

"No, no," gurgled Sea, "I'm having far too much fun. Find someone else to do your dirty work, you silly little bird!" Sparrow flapped her wings with rage.

"You'll be sorry, Sea!" she squawked. "I'm going to get Elephant to drink you up – every single drop!"

Sparrow flew furiously back into the forest. There she found Elephant under the trees, enjoying her afternoon nap.

"Oi!" cried Sparrow, jumping up and down on Elephant's enormous back. "Wake up! I've got an important job for you. Go and drink up all the Sea."

Elephant opened her eyes and lumbered slowly to her feet.

"Drink the sea, Sparrow?" she rumbled. "Yuck! The Sea's so salty, just one mouthful of her would make me sick."

"*Please*, Elephant," begged Sparrow, "just do it as a favour for me."

But Elephant shook her head, lay down again and went back to sleep.

"You'll be sorry, Elephant!" cried Sparrow. "I'm going to get the fiercest creature in the whole world to bite you!"

Elephant chuckled. A big, fat thing like her wasn't afraid of anything.

However, Elephant had no idea what Sparrow meant by 'the fiercest creature in the whole world'. Can you guess what it was?

The angry little bird went fluttering through the trees, calling softly:

"Mosquito, Mosquito, where are you? Can you help me?"

And at once, Mosquito came.

"Zzzzzzzz," she hummed, "what can I do for you, friend Sparrow?"

"Elephant's annoying me," said Sparrow. "I want you to bite her ear hard."

And at once Mosquito cried, "I will!"

"Zzzzzzz!" Mosquito came humming boldly through the trees, getting closer and closer to Elephant.

Elephant jumped up in a panic. She was terrified at the thought of a nasty, swollen, itchy mosquito bite!

"Stop!" she bellowed. "Please don't bite me, Mosquito! I'll drink Sea after all!"

She lumbered down to the shore and put out her trunk. But before she could drink a single drop, Sea darted away and gurgled,

"Don't drink me!
I promise I'll put out
Fire!"

But before Sea could reach Fire, he crackled,
"Don't put me out! I'm just about to burn Stick!"

"No!" cried Stick, jumping away from the flames. "Don't burn me! I promise I'll beat Dog!"

"Oh no you won't!" growled Dog, "because I'm going to gobble up Mouse!"

He got ready to pounce; but Mouse scuttled away, squeaking:
"Please don't, please don't! Look, I'm off to chew Mr Woodcutter's clothes!"

"Get off, you silly Mouse!" yelled the woodcutter. "Can't you see? I'm on my way to cut down Tree. That will get rid of nasty, selfish Crow!"

He picked up his axe and got ready to swing it.

"Help!" roared Tree.

The axe came gleaming through the sunlight towards him...

But before the axe could touch Tree's trunk, Crow squawked, "Stop!" and flew to the ground, carrying the pearl. He looked very embarrassed.

"Don't cut Tree down," Crow whispered. "Look! I've come out of it all by myself."

He dropped the pearl at Sparrow's feet. "Here you are, friend. Is this what you wanted?"

"Yes," answered Sparrow, whispering too.

"WHAT A STUPID FUSS ABOUT NOTHING!" shouted Mosquito, Elephant, Sea, Fire, Stick, Dog, Mouse, Woodcutter and Tree.

"Sorry," said Sparrow.

"So am I," said Crow.

The two birds hopped slowly towards each other and touched beaks. And after that day, they never, ever argued again.